ADVENTURES
~ OF THE ~
SHARK LADY

Eugenie Clark
Around the World

ADVENTURES
~ OF THE ~
SHARK LADY

Eugenie Clark
Around the World

by
Ann McGovern

SCHOLASTIC INC.
New York Toronto London Auckland Sydney

Photograph credits: Front cover, Chuck Davis/IMAX Film Production; back cover, Nikki Konstantinou; p. x, Marty Scheiner; p. 9, Stan Waterman; pp. 14, 68, Nikki Konstantinou; p. 18, David Doubilet; pp. 35, 53, Emory Kristof/National Geographic Image Collection; p. 62, Eugene K. Balon

Pages from Eugenie Clark's notebooks, pp. 33, 46, 56, courtesy of Eugenie Clark

ISBN 0-590-45712-8

12 11 10 9 8 7 6 5   2 3/0

Printed in the U.S.A.   40

First Scholastic printing, April 1998

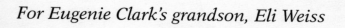

For Eugenie Clark's grandson, Eli Weiss

Contents

EUGENIE IN THE DEEP, DEEP SEA

FAMOUS EUGENIE CLARK

Meet Eugenie Clark

Dear Reader,

Eugenie Clark's story began when she was nine years old and visited the New York Aquarium for the first time. Eugenie was fascinated by the fish she saw there, especially the biggest ones — the sharks. Soon Eugenie was going to the aquarium every week.

As her fascination grew, she asked her mother to help her set up her own aquarium at home. Before long, their small apartment was crowded with fish of all kinds. In college,

Ann McGovern and Eugenie Clark

she studied different creatures. She learned how to *dissect*, or cut up, dead animals.

Once, a friendly pet shop owner gave Eugenie a dead monkey. She took it home and put it in the refrigerator so it wouldn't spoil and smell bad. When her grandmother opened the refrigerator and saw the dead monkey on the shelf, she screamed, "No more dead animals in this house!" And there weren't — until the day Eugenie wanted the skeleton of a big dead rat. She used one of her grandmother's pots to boil the rat!

Eugenie became a marine biologist when she grew up. On a trip to study poisonous fish in the South Seas, she found herself swimming far from shore. She sensed something behind her. It was a big shark and it was swimming right toward her! Eugenie knew she should be frightened. But she wasn't. All she could do was admire the shark.

That first meeting with a shark became a lifelong interest. She learned to scuba dive so she could stay in the underwater world for over an hour at a time, studying the habits of the fish on a reef.

Eugenie became a world-famous scientist, professor, and the director of a laboratory in Florida, where she successfully kept sharks in captivity. The most interesting part of her work was studying live sharks. She got to know the sharks so well that she could tell one from another by their behavior. She learned about their feeding habits, that sharks were smart enough to learn simple tasks, and that they had a good memory.

My book *Shark Lady, True Adventures of Eugenie Clark* tells about many of Eugenie's early adventures with sharks. More than twenty years have gone by since the book was written. Over the years, Eugenie has had even more adventures that have taken her all over the world.

In this book you will read about the Shark Lady's most exciting and dangerous dives and about the important discoveries she has made that have helped us all learn more about the fascinating world of the sea and its creatures.

Ann McGovern

New York, New York

EUGENIE AROUND
THE WORLD

*Eugenie has scuba dived and lectured
around the world. Look at the map
on the next page and see all
the places she's been!*

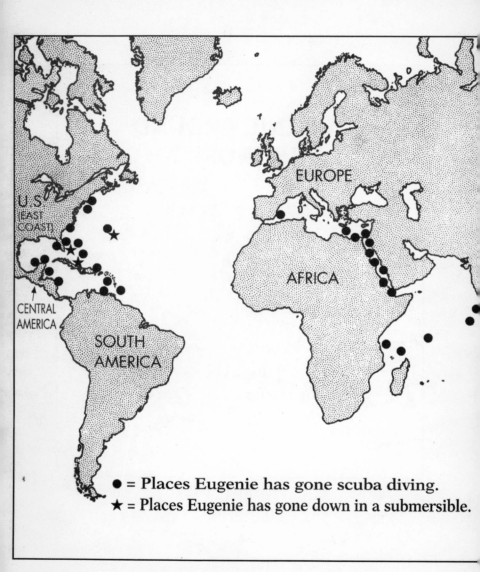

● = Places Eugenie has gone scuba diving.
★ = Places Eugenie has gone down in a submersible.

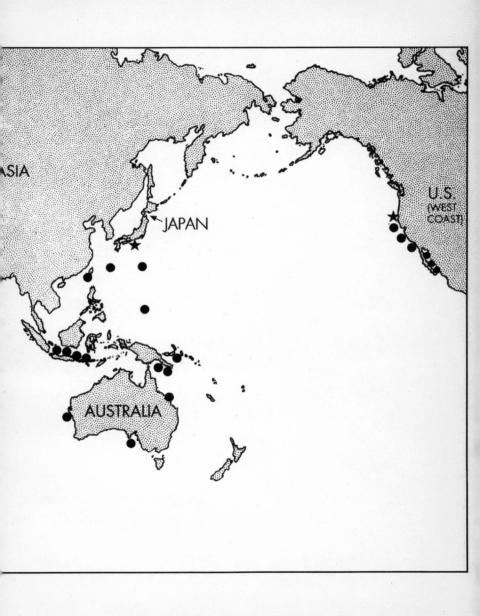

1
Diving with
Great White Sharks

The great white shark rushed straight toward Eugenie, its mouth wide open. The shark's mighty jaws crunched down on steel bars, a few inches from Eugenie's face. She pressed against the far side of the steel shark cage only to feel another great white shark's nose poking through the cage at her back.

It was 1979 and Dr. Eugenie Clark had come to Dangerous Reef in South Australia to study the great white shark up close. Of all the different kinds of sharks, the great white is the one that strikes the most fear in people's hearts.

Eugenie was with photographer David Doubilet and his wife, Anne. Rodney Fox, an Australian diver, had made all the arrangements. He chartered the boat and equipped it with steel cages that were designed to hold divers underwater and protect them from the sharks.

Anne, David, and Eugenie examined the cages closely.

"You may think they look frail," Rodney Fox said. "But they do the job. We haven't lost anybody" — he grinned — "yet!"

Eugenie had made hundreds of dives with different kinds of sharks around the world. But the great white shark was different.

"It's the only shark whose diet is made up of objects as large as humans," she said.

"Did you say humans?" David said. "Hey, that's what we are."

"The great white shark has rarely — if ever — eaten an entire human being," Eugenie said. "It uses the bite-and-spit-out method. Of course, if the bite is big enough, you could lose an arm or a leg, or enough blood to die.

But the great white sharks prefer a meal of other fish, octopuses, and sea lions."

Eugenie knew what kept great whites around Dangerous Reef. There was a big colony of sea lions, a favorite meal for the big sharks. Rodney also threw *chum* into the water — huge amounts of blood, meat, and tuna — to bring in the great whites.

Underwater, Eugenie and David were in two separate cages side by side, only ten feet apart. Eugenie had brought her own camera. The great white sharks charged and pounded at the two cages. The cages shook! Steel met steel as sharks more than fourteen feet long kept charging at them. One minute the cages clanged together. The next minute, a shark charged between them and the cages were knocked apart.

Eugenie and David caught glimpses of each other's wide-eyed expressions through their face masks as the sharks crashed against the cages. At one time, they were in the water with five great white sharks swimming around them!

The charging and thrusting were only a small part of the sharks' reaction to the strange human invaders. Most of the time they swam past the cages, so streamlined, so graceful that Eugenie was awestruck by their beauty.

Then suddenly all the sharks disappeared. In the strange silence, Eugenie kept turning slowly around in her cage, wondering from which direction the next shark would come. In a way this was the spookiest part of the adventure.

It wasn't long before a shark came. Instead of backing against the far side of the cage, she aimed her camera in its face when it swam head-on. Sometimes she even reached through the bars and managed to stroke one as it passed.

Eugenie spent ten days at Dangerous Reef with David, Anne, and Rodney Fox. From the underwater cages, David shot picture after picture of great white sharks. Eugenie made notes about their behavior. To lure the sharks, Rodney kept dumping the blood and ground-up tuna bait into the sea. For good measure, he hung chunks of meat under the boat. Often, when Eugenie was in her shark cage, Rodney poured another messy load overboard and Eugenie would get a shampoo of blood and guts!

Eugenie remembered that, years ago, the great underwater explorer William Beebe called sharks "chinless cowards." Beebe knew, as most experienced scuba divers know, that sharks are usually frightened away by people. But not the great white. Eugenie says, "No amount of commotion, of people taking pictures or whooping and yelling, seems to affect it. When it's lured to the boat by the chum, it's the only shark that actually comes to the surface, sticks its head out, and seems to look the boat over."

On the last night, Eugenie and her friends were enjoying a late supper when they heard a heavy thump at the back of the boat. A massive great white was ramming the boat as it stole a fifty-pound bag of tuna bait hanging on the platform, well above the water.

The shark thumped the boat all night, slapping it with its tail and actually lifting the thirty-two-foot boat from below.

Eugenie left Dangerous Reef with the conviction that the great white sharks must be protected. People kill the great whites for their fins and tails for soup! They get over thirty dollars a pound. And a set of jaws from a really big shark can go for as much as one thousand dollars. At the rate sharks are being hunted, there won't be any big ones left.

"If the number of great white sharks, or any shark for that matter, is greatly reduced by overfishing, it could change the ecology of the oceans," Eugenie says. "It would be a tragedy if such a magnificent animal vanished forever from the oceans of the world."

2
Riding the
Giant Whale Shark

In 1983, Eugenie was invited to Mexico's Sea of Cortez to dive with whale sharks, the biggest fish in the sea. The wind was blowing like a gale. Eugenie and her friends wondered if they'd ever be able to get in the water with a whale shark.

For six days, Eugenie and her friends waited in safe harbor for the winds to die down. They talked and dreamed of whale sharks, the gentle giants of the sea.

At last the weather changed. Now the pilot could take the spotter plane up to see if there were whale sharks below.

"Whale shark right in front of you!" the pilot announced on his radiophone.

Quickly Eugenie and her friends put on their scuba gear and plunged into the path of a whale shark.

It looks like a spaceship, Eugenie thought as she got close to the harmless monster. Dozens of small remoras were clinging to the whale shark, under its chin, and inside its mouth and gill slits. Remoras are fish that travel with big fish to eat their leftovers and clean parasites off the sharks' skin.

One of the filmmakers moved in front of the shark, and Eugenie could see just how huge the whale shark truly was. The six-foot man looked like a tiny doll next to the shark.

The whale shark paid no attention to the divers. It didn't try to swim away. But even so, Eugenie had to struggle to catch up.

Almost out of breath, she reached out and felt its hard, thick skin. Then she grabbed the whale shark's big back dorsal fin and held onto it as the whale shark continued its downward plunge.

A whale shark takes Eugenie for a ride.

Down, down it went. Twenty-five feet, thirty feet. A hundred feet.

With Eugenie still hanging on, the great shark tilted its head and slid into the depths, as if to say "Let me take you to where no human has ever gone."

The shark continued its slow-motion ride toward an unseen bottom. Deeper it went and deeper still. At last Eugenie began to feel drugged, the dangerous effect of nitrogen narcosis that deep-water divers experience at extreme depths.

At 185 feet, she had to let go.

Back on the surface, Eugenie and her friends were bubbling with excitement. "If I were a remora," Eugenie said, "I would love to ride on this whale shark forever!"

3
Whale Sharks
at Ningaloo Reef

It was March of 1991, eight years after Eugenie rode a whale shark in Mexico. She was on a *National Geographic* assignment at Ningaloo Reef in Western Australia, halfway around the world from her home. The photographer David Doubilet was with her. They came here to photograph and learn more about the rare and spectacular whale shark. Ningaloo Reef is Western Australia's biggest marine park, and all fish, including the whale shark, are protected here.

Out of the deep blue gloom, a whale shark swam toward them, all thirty feet and ten tons of it. David moved in front of the giant fish to photograph its enormous mouth as it was feeding. He was not afraid of the huge shark. Whale sharks don't eat large animals like people. They feed on small fish and plankton, mainly shrimplike krill.

By the end of the day, Eugenie and David had seen twenty whale sharks. They were overjoyed. Many marine scientists have never even found one.

Eugenie was at Ningaloo Reef at the right time. The conditions were ideal for whale sharks. About a week after the March full moon is when corals spawn. Corals contain thousands and thousands of living animals called *polyps*. Coral spawning happens when millions of tiny eggs and sperm pop out of the polyps. Then dense schools of small fish are attracted to this "plankton soup."

Eugenie had never before dived during a coral spawning. "It's like being at a party celebration, where everyone releases miniature pink and white balloons," she said.

After the spawning, it wasn't long before

whales, manta rays, and the whale sharks arrived to feed.

Eugenie is fascinated by the whale shark's feeding behavior. It swims slowly on the surface toward a dense mass of plankton with tiny fish. As it swims through the ball of food, it moves its head from side to side, sucking in its food. "It looks like someone using a vacuum cleaner in the corners," David said. Sometimes the whale shark comes almost to a complete stop. It hangs with its tail down, pumping up and down in the water as the plankton soup is sucked into its mouth, like water running down the drain in a bathtub.

At Ningaloo Reef, David warned Eugenie about diving too deep. "Remember," David said, "we've got lots of whale sharks around. Stay near the surface so I can get the best light for pictures. Don't go below fifty feet! Check your depth gauge!"

Eugenie caught onto the dorsal fin of a young twenty-foot whale shark. The clean design of its white spots reminded Eugenie of a set of dark blue-and-white dominoes. David

Eugenie writes underwater with a special pen and pad.

was looking through the viewfinder of his camera, lost in taking close-up portraits of the shark's head. Eugenie and the shark swam down. Eugenie felt she was being towed through the water by a living submarine. Then she checked her depth gauge. She and David were already below a hundred feet! Twice as deep as they meant to go. They headed for the surface, happy with their whale shark dive.

In a month, the two divers saw two hundred whale sharks — more than Eugenie ever dreamed possible in a lifetime. They began to recognize individual whale sharks by their scars, line patterns, and spots.

Once Eugenie dissected a whale shark. She was amazed to find that the brain of a whale shark is just behind its upper lip.

She and David studied whale sharks up close and from the boat. David even got a photograph of two whale sharks together — each more than twenty-five feet long, weighing about nine tons. One whale shark was over thirty feet long. David climbed onto its head and aimed his camera right into the shark's mouth!

Are the whale sharks bothered? From her experiences, Eugenie thinks that large whale sharks don't mind contact with divers, but young ones may be disturbed.

Today, a great many divers go to Ningaloo Reef to see the whale sharks. They can swim with the sharks, but they are asked not to ride or touch them.

4
Shark Lady in the Grip
of a Monster Crab

Once again, Eugenie and photographer David Doubilet were on assignment for *National Geographic*. They were writing and photographing a story on Japan's Izu Oceanic Park, home of the giant spider crab.

David needed a good picture of the crab for the story. He was thrilled to find a big one on the sand, 140 feet below the sea.

No one had ever photographed the giant crab so deep in the ocean.

David gave Eugenie an underwater signal. Eugenie understood that he wanted her to come closer and lift the crab's head so that he

Eugenie grabs the head of the giant spider crab.

could get a great photo. The only way Eugenie could raise the monster's head was to get behind it and reach over its back. So scuba tank and all, she crept up behind the crab, dug her flippers into the sand, and pulled up the crab's head.

Neither she nor David could have imagined what would happen next.

The crab didn't want its head pulled up. It tried to put its head down but it needed to brace itself against something — and the only thing close at hand was Eugenie's leg!

18

The giant spider crab wrapped one of its legs around Eugenie's thigh, then another around her other leg.

This was no ordinary crab that was holding Eugenie prisoner below the sea. It was a member of the largest crab species in the world and found only in Japan. From the tip of one outstretched claw to the other, these crabs grow to twelve feet across, the size of two tall men, lying end to end. Its stalked eyes move independently and look forward, backward, and sideways.

Trapped by a giant crab! She thought of what the Japanese call this monster — *shinin gani* — dead man's crab. It is known to feed on the bodies of people who drown in the sea.

Quickly she put that thought out of her mind and concentrated on freeing the crab's tight grip on her legs. Each time she pulled its head up a little, the crab pulled down as if they were playing a game of strength. She managed to unlock one of the crab's legs from her thigh. Still holding onto the crab's head, she struggled to get her other leg free.

Divers were holding big lights so that David could get his picture. Eugenie felt like she was on a stage and that she and the crab were the stars of some weird movie. She laughed to herself as she thought of a movie title: *Shark Lady in the Grip of a Monster Crab!*

The divers had only a few more minutes before they had to start up to the surface. They were in danger of getting the "bends," the dreaded disease that scuba divers who dive too deep for too long can get. The bends can be crippling or even fatal.

The crab started to walk sideways, carrying Eugenie away from the lights and camera. The crab was heading straight for the rocks! But it didn't bash Eugenie against them. Now it could hold onto the rocks, not Eugenie's legs, as leverage against her. Eugenie could no longer hold the crab's face up for the camera and the crab let her go.

As long as Eugenie lives, she will remember her adventure with the Japanese giant spider crab!

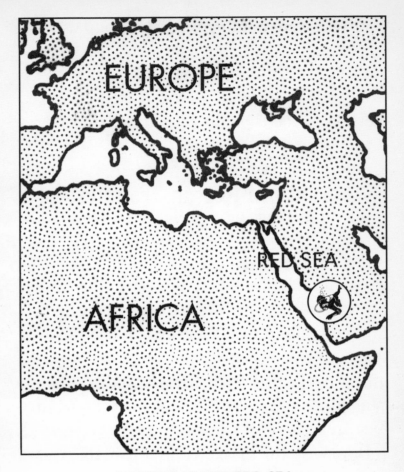

EUGENIE IN THE RED SEA

Here is where Eugenie likes to go scuba diving every summer to study sharks and other fantastic creatures in the Red Sea.

5
A Coral Reef in Trouble!

Eugenie Clark floated down in the water. She was in Egypt, at her favorite reef, Ras Mohammed. It was her first scuba dive of the summer of 1980. She couldn't wait to greet her favorite fish friends and the beautiful corals of the Red Sea. Soon she was fifty feet deep.

Here were the masked puffer fish, the parrot fish, and the long-nosed banded pipefish. Here were the lionfishes, their fins tipped with poison. She dove through forests of big pink sea fans and swam past colorful corals that looked like they belonged in a fairy tale. A streamlined silvertip shark swam by. The tiny clown fish made her laugh.

Except for the fishes, what she saw on the reef this day did not make her laugh. She almost wept at the sight of junk and garbage strewn all over: anchors, ropes, tin cans and bottles, and hundreds of yards of nylon fishing lines and hooks.

Eugenie and her diving friends decided to have an underwater cleanup day. They took bags and bags of junk out of the sea. But the cleanup was only a drop in the bucket. Eugenie knew that something more had to be done to save the reefs. Ras Mohammed was in grave danger of becoming an underwater dump, a watery wasteland.

Eugenie remembered the first time she dove at Ras Mohammed. In 1950, fishermen and sailors told Eugenie it was a place of fabulous reefs and vast numbers of fishes. In the 1960s, Eugenie and her friends started going there by bumpy Jeep, for there were no real roads.

Over the years Eugenie began to see changes at Ras Mohammed. By 1978, it had become one of the most popular dive sites in the world. Thousands of scuba divers, campers, fishermen, scientists, vacationers, and photographers drove down new roads to get to the beautiful reefs. Boats took divers out. Then an airport was built nearby and people flew in from around the world.

Vacationers dumped their garbage into the sea. Heavy debris tumbled down Ras Mohammed's steep reef walls. Garbage spread over the once beautiful shores.

And that wasn't all. Fishermen changed from cotton to the stronger nylon fishing lines that weren't biodegradable. Their lines and hooks caught on living coral. As they pulled the lines up, big chunks of coral were broken up. Some fishermen even used dynamite to blast the reefs to kill fish. They dropped their anchors, which smashed into the coral reefs. In a few seconds, living coral formations were broken apart — some coral formations that scientists say take up to two thousand years to form.

Thousands of years to grow, Eugenie thought. And only seconds to die.

Eugenie knew that something had to be done. But what? In 1980, Eugenie met a young Egyptian diver, Gamal Sadat. He introduced Eugenie to his father. Gamal's father was the president of Egypt. Eugenie lost no time in telling President Sadat about the marvels of Ras Mohammed.

"Is it true that Egypt owns one of the most beautiful coral reefs in the world?" President Sadat asked.

Then Eugenie told Sadat about the threat to these reefs. To her great surprise, he said, "I will make Ras Mohammed a national park. That way it can be protected forever." His eyes twinkled. "But I have one condition," he said. "You must promise to protect my son from the man-eating sharks."

Gamal smiled. "My father watches *Jaws* too much. It's one of his favorite movies."

6
The Fight to Save
Ras Mohammed

Eugenie could hardly believe her success with the president of Egypt. Preparations for the national park were started immediately.

But by the end of the year everything changed. In 1981, President Sadat was killed by an assassin's bullet! Ras Mohammed Marine Park was forgotten.

Eugenie did not give up. She got her diving friends to write letters to the new president of Egypt. Conservation groups around the world joined in to save Ras Mohammed.

While Eugenie and her Egyptian friend Ayman Taher were making a movie, *Treasures of Ras Mohammed,* Eugenie learned to her horror that a big fishing tournament was about to begin there. Sport fishermen and their boat anchors, fishing lines, and hooks would destroy more coral reefs.

Eugenie and Ayman rushed to where the opening ceremonies were being held. The party had already begun. On the tables were the prizes and medals to be given out at the end of the three-day tournament. The man in charge was Sayed Marei, a former prime minister. He was about to give a speech to open the ceremonies when he noticed a lovely, small, dark-haired woman running up to him.

"And what can I do for you?" Sayed asked.

"I'd like you to stop the fishing tournament!" Eugenie said in a strong, determined voice.

Sayed Marei's wife and sister, standing next to him, could hardly believe Eugenie's request. They were dressed in their best clothes for the ceremony. Just who was this American woman in jeans, a T-shirt, and sandals?

But they listened intently as Eugenie began to tell them how terrible it would be for Ras Mohammed if the boats anchored and fished there. She told them about the underwater wonders that needed to be saved.

"Are you the American professor President Sadat told me about?" Sayed Marei asked.

Eugenie nodded.

"Well, young lady," he said, laughing. "You told President Sadat about the thousands of fish at Ras Mohammed. That's exactly why we're holding the fishing tournament here!"

Eugenie convinced Sayed Marei to keep the fishermen out of Ras Mohammed. He moved the tournament to a site where reefs would not be damaged. Most important, Sayed Marei convinced his friends in government to save Ras Mohammed. In 1983, Ras Mohammed became the first national park of Egypt. It was the first time any country made a marine park its first national park.

But Eugenie soon learned that Ras Mohammed was still in danger. There was very little money to plan and manage the new park. There was no way to make the laws stick that would protect the reefs.

Fishing with nylon lines and dynamite went on as before. There wasn't one official to stop anyone from spearing fish and taking lobsters. Shell and coral collectors stripped the reefs close to shore.

Eugenie felt very discouraged. But in the summer of 1989, she saw a real breakthrough. The new people in charge of the national park were scuba divers. They understood marine life and how to protect the beautiful reefs in their trust.

When Eugenie got back to her home in Maryland at the end of that summer, she took part in an important meeting in Washington, D.C. Seven underwater "wonders of the world" were to be selected as a way to call attention to the urgent need for worldwide marine conservation. Ras Mohammed was voted one of the seven wonders.

But today, Eugenie is afraid that Ras

Mohammed is once again in danger of being spoiled by an ever-growing number of visitors. "It takes constant care and attention to keep the coral reef beautiful," she says. She hopes that Ras Mohammed will not become an underwater dump again.

7
One Discovery Leads to Another

Eugenie checked her scuba tank's air supply. Good. She had enough air to stay an hour more at thirty feet below the sea to study the colony of garden eels that live in the sand.

She was looking closely at a garden eel when she saw a few sand grains jumping around like crazy, like the start of a miniature volcanic eruption. She collected some of the jumping sand grains, and back in her lab she looked at them under a microscope. She found that tiny creatures live under the sand grains. They stick together bits of shells and grains of sand to build a tiny "house" that they carry along as they hop.

Studying the sand grains led to the study of other sand fish, like the Ninja fish that disappears into the sand in the blink of an eye.

One night at Ras Mohammed, after watching the mating behavior of reef sharks, Eugenie got out of the water and removed her dive gear. The moon had not yet risen. Before going into her tent on the shores of the Red Sea to write up her notes, she looked out over the dark waters. She saw lights blinking on and off in the night sea. The lights came from fish the size of little goldfish. They were *Photoblepharon*, or flashlight fish.

The light comes from billions of tiny glowing bacteria that live in the pockets under the fish's eyes. Here's where the "flash" comes from: When the fish wants to turn off its light, it raises a black-out skin covering. And when it wants to turn its light on again, it lowers the covering. Flashlight fish use their lights to attract food, confuse their enemies, and signal one another.

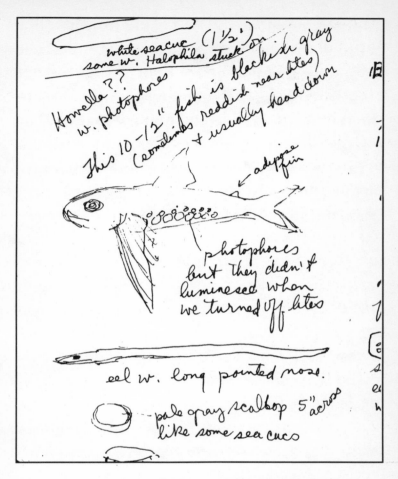

A page from Eugenie Clark's notebooks

Eugenie sketched some of the creatures she saw on a dive in the Bahamas. Like the flashlight fish in Ras Mohammed, one of the fish she saw has photophores that light up. They are along the bottom of the fish's body.

"Swimming with these flashlight fish is like drifting with twinkling jack-o'-lanterns," she says, "or glowing mystery lights."

Every summer, Eugenie tries to return to the Red Sea with friends. And every time they learn something new!

Eugenie never has to worry about what project she'll study next. Every new discovery leads to more scientific puzzles to solve.

EUGENIE IN THE DEEP, DEEP SEA

Eugenie Clark has been the scientist in charge of seventy-one submersible dives and has made fifty-one deep-sea dives herself. In submersibles, such as the Pisces, *she has gone down to depths from 1,000 to 12,000 feet to study the behavior of deep-sea fish, especially sharks.*

8
Down to 2,000 Feet

Down, down, off the coast of Bermuda in the Atlantic Ocean, the submersible sank. It plunged three hundred feet every five minutes. Eugenie Clark peered through the plastic window, fascinated by the strange underwater world. Thousands of tiny creatures, the size of sugar crystals, formed a cloud of reddish sparks. Worms dashed through the cloud like shooting stars. A silvery blue fish, only three inches long, shot into view. It stood on its head and began to bounce like a pogo stick.

Eugenie checked her watch. She could hardly believe half an hour had passed so quickly! Just a little while ago she was at sea level, safely aboard the fishing boat *Miss Wendy*.

Now Eugenie, the submersible pilot, and Emory Kristof of the National Geographic Society were cramped in the small sub *Pisces VI*. Emory was too tall to stand up straight in the six-foot sphere. Much of the space was taken up with instruments.

"In only a few minutes, I've gone deeper than I've ever been using scuba," Eugenie realized.

The pilot's announcement interrupted her excited thoughts.

"*Pisces VI* to *Miss Wendy*. We are at one thousand feet. One zero, zero, zero."

Light flashed in the inky waters. Emory was grinning. His videos and cameras were working fine, lighting up a saber-toothed viper fish with fangs as long as its head. And a silvery hatchet fish was gleaming like tinsel.

Like Alice in an underwater wonderland, Eugenie peered through the "looking glass" of *Pisces VI*.

"*Pisces VI* to *Miss Wendy*. We are passing thirteen hundred feet. One, three, zero, zero," the pilot said into the radio.

Eugenie began to feel cold and clammy.

Oh, no, she thought. She looked at the walls of the sub and saw droplets of water.

Could the submersible be leaking? was her first terrible thought. She turned to the pilot who didn't look at all worried.

"It's cold outside at this depth," the pilot said. "The warm air and our breath is turning into water and it's dripping down the cold walls."

Eugenie took out a warm jacket from the bag she had brought on board. Inside the bag were three chocolate bars, a cheese sandwich, and a plastic mayonnaise jar. There was no room for a bathroom in the sub. That was what the mayonnaise jar was for. She also had a notebook and pen to record everything she saw.

The pilot spotted a good place to set the submersible down. For a moment the sub hovered like a spacecraft about to land on the moon. Then it settled down on the bottom.

"*Pisces VI* to *Miss Wendy*," the pilot said. "We have landed at two thousand feet. Two, zero, zero, zero."

Eugenie shivered with excitement. Two thousand feet down to inky blackness. Five hundred children standing on each other's shoulders would be about two thousand feet.

The pilot turned off the lights inside the sub. "We're really on the bottom of the sea!" His words echoed Eugenie's excited thoughts.

It was lucky that Eugenie was not a worrier. She knew about the possible dangers. The batteries of the submersible could die. Or the sub could spring a leak that would mean instant death. But she trusted this submersible. It had made hundreds of deep dives safely.

Eugenie peered through the window at the night world outside, dimly lit by glowing green chemical sticks that were tied to the cage being carried down by the mechanical arm of the submersible. The cage was baited with tuna to lure in creatures of the deep. It was placed in front of the sub.

Eugenie had studied and worked with many

shallow-water sharks all over the world. Now she might see the deep-sea sharks: the giant six-gill shark; the tiny cookie-cutter shark, which leaves a round cookie-cutter mark on its victims; the rare huge megamouth shark; or the goblin shark, which no one had ever seen alive.

A large eye with a fish's body loomed in the distance. It was too far away for Eugenie to tell what it was. The eye shone like a cat's eye, reflecting the dim light.

Suddenly she heard a noise, like teeth chomping on metal. The sub rocked and lifted slightly. "It was nudged from below by a creature of enormous strength," she wrote in an article for *National Geographic*. "Then this huge broad head came from underneath the sub. And the green eye of a shark was looking in as if looking at me."

It was a huge six-gill shark. "It must be eighteen feet!" Emory said. "As big as a truck!"

As it battered the submersible, Eugenie had her first chance to observe this speckled deepwater shark so close. It had parasites hanging from its fins, like babies riding a magic carpet.

She wrote pages of notes, describing every detail of the new creatures. "The sharks move as in a dream or a slow-motion movie," she wrote. She drew pictures of the strange world 2,000 feet deep. The tapioca fish, never before seen alive, "looks like a huge, chocolate barracuda," she wrote. It had big teeth and a hook on each scale.

Four hours had gone by. It was time to go up. Eugenie had completely lost track of time in the eerie blackness that stretched out forever.

Before they reached the surface, Emory was planning the next submersible dive. What other marvels lay waiting for them in the depths of the sea?

9
Another Dream Come True

Back on *Miss Wendy,* Eugenie and Emory felt it had been a dream come true for both of them. Emory had gotten first-ever photos and movies of giant sharks in the deep sea.

And another one of Eugenie's dreams had come true.

In 1934, when Eugenie was eleven years old, scientist William Beebe was her hero. He went half a mile beneath the sea in an underwater craft called a *bathysphere.* He described a fantastic new world and creatures with huge fangs and hinged mouths. He wrote about them in books and magazine articles that Eugenie read. Eugenie felt she was right there with him. She dreamed of someday exploring these hidden depths, of seeing what Beebe saw.

Now, more than half a century later, she had actually seen the creatures he described! The hatchet fish, the viper fish, and the deep-sea eels. And fishes that Dr. Beebe had never seen — like the sharks.

The fishing boat, *Miss Wendy*, belonged to her friend Teddy Tucker, a shipwreck explorer and deep-sea fisherman who lived in Bermuda. Teddy got the idea of attaching the green glowing chemical sticks to his fishing lines. Fishes were attracted by those glowing lights. They looked like *photophores*, the light organs of deep-sea fishes that lured in their prey.

Teddy and another local fisherman, Blue-Eye Billy, knew about the deep places in the sea where the rare four-eyed sharks swam. And where there were many big six-gill sharks.

Up to now, no one had actually seen the big sharks swimming in the deep sea. When submersibles go down to repair oil lines, they carry lights but no bait. Their bright underwater lights shine only on an empty sea bottom.

William Beebe hadn't seen any deep-sea sharks either, when he went half a mile down in 1934. He wasn't able to land on the bottom where sharks dwell. The cable holding his bathysphere might tangle in cliffs or debris. He described the bathysphere as "a pea dangling in the sea, hanging by a spidery thread." He never carried a bait cage.

It was Emory's idea to use a submersible as a "blind," or hiding place. He wanted to carry fish bait in cages to bring in the creatures of the deep and photograph them.

With Teddy Tucker's help, Emory started the Beebe Project, named after Eugenie's childhood hero. Eugenie joined the Beebe Project as chief scientist, and a new phase of her exciting career began.

It took over a year of planning, designing, and testing. Emory attached cameras on the sub. The bait cage was loaded with chunks of dead fish and bloody fish guts. The cage was carried down by the mechanical arm of the submersible. The green glowing chemical sticks were tied to the bait cage. When the sub reached the bottom, the arm dropped the bait cage. Then the pilot turned off the lights and backed the sub away to get a wider view of the creatures that came to the cage.

After a while, the sharks came in, attracted by the green glow and the fishy smells from the bait cage.

From 1987 to 1990, Eugenie was in charge of seventy-one submersible dives. She made fifty-one of the dives herself. Her deepest dive was in the U.S. submersible *Alvin,* to 12,000 feet — more than two miles down! Her longest dive was seventeen and a half hours, in the Russian submersible *Mir,* which means "peace."

Eugenie explored the deep sea in eight different submersibles made in four different countries. She dove off the coasts of Bermuda,

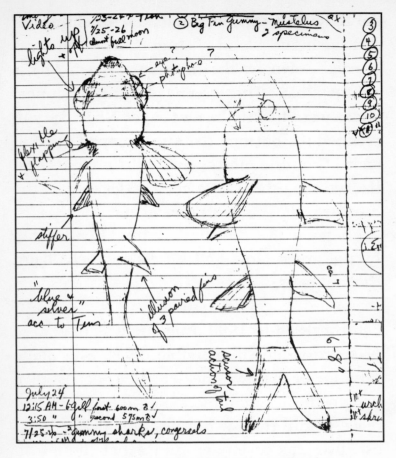

A page from Eugenie Clark's notebooks

On one dive in Bermuda, Eugenie saw six-gill and bigfin gummy sharks — and a fish she could not identify. She made two drawings of the 6 - 8 foot long "mystery" fish in her notebook. She could tell this was a bony fish, not a shark, which has cartilage instead of bone.

the Bahamas, the Cayman Islands, California, and Japan.

Eugenie and Emory saw the biggest living six-gill sharks, the cookie-cutter shark, and the tapioca fish in the deep sea. Eugenie also saw gulper sharks, glowing lantern sharks, bigfin gummy sharks, cat sharks, and cigar sharks.

In her notebooks, she recorded new scientific information.

Eugenie is looking forward to more deep dives. She dreams about the mysteries of this deep dark world and of learning more about the strange creatures who live there.

10
Danger Below

Every submersible dive was fascinating to Eugenie. One dark, moonless night in 1989, she was down three thousand feet off Grand Cayman Island in the Caribbean. The submersible was sitting on a ledge of an underwater cliff.

"Okay, Eugenie," the pilot said. "Take your last notes. It's time to go up."

Eugenie hated to leave. She was watching eels standing on their heads, and taking notes about ghostly fish that looked like giant tadpoles.

The submersible started to move. Eugenie peered out of the window.

"We're going down, not up!" she said. Tiny particles in the water always fell like snow, on the way up. But now, Eugenie saw that the particles were going up, not down!

"We're going down!" she said again. "Check your gauge!"

"I hate to tell you," the pilot said in a worried voice, "but the depth gauge is broken. And the backup depth gauge is out, too. I don't know what's pulling us down. I'll have to release the emergency ballast weight." When the weight is released, the sub immediately gets lighter and goes up.

The pilot pulled the release lever. Nothing happened. He pulled harder. It was stuck!

The pilot began to sweat. He struggled with the lever. He fiddled with the gauges. Nothing worked.

They were at unrecorded depths and it was now midnight.

Far above them was a motorboat, its captain watching a bright light bobbing on the surface. The light was attached to the top of the submersible by a long line. That's how the captain of the motorboat kept track of the submersible. Suddenly the captain could not see the light. Where was the submersible? How far down was it? What had gone wrong?

Beneath the sea, Eugenie felt the submersible turn, first to the right, then to the left, as though a giant hand were pushing them around.

Eugenie remembered what another submersible pilot once said to her. "I'm not afraid of anything that can happen in a sub, except getting tangled in lines or cables. Then we're in *big* trouble."

Eugenie was beginning to feel frightened. The submersible continued to bump and sway, moving from left to right, right to left. Bump, bang. Bang, bump.

Eugenie knew they could have stayed down longer. The submersible carried a water emergency system and enough spare air to last three more days. But it was cold and damp and cramped down there. And they were out of food. Eugenie didn't even have any more candy bars.

Suddenly the submersible stopped bumping. They began to go up. Eugenie breathed a sigh of relief. The pilot stopped sweating. Forty-five minutes later, they reached the surface. The motorboat zoomed up to greet them.

They figured out the reason for their predicament. The line attached to the sub had indeed snagged under a rocky ledge! That's why the sub was bumping so much. The light that was attached to the line got pulled under the sea. Finally the line unsnagged and the sub was free to start up.

Never in all the dozens of dives Eugenie had made had anything like this happened. She never wanted it to happen again.

In the years and dives that followed, nothing ever went wrong.

11
Shark Lady Meets Monsters
of the Deep

Eugenie pressed her face hard against the porthole of the submersible. She could hardly believe her eyes. A mass of six-gill sharks had appeared from the gloom of the deep sea and were slowly circling the bait cage.

"Look!" the pilot of the sub shouted. "They're fighting!" A female shark, about twelve feet long, was pulling itself out of a male six-gill shark's mouth. Eugenie could barely see the marks on the female's head where the male had chomped down.

"No, the sharks aren't fighting," Eugenie told the pilot. "They had their mouths open,

Emory Kristof took this picture right after a male six-gill shark grabbed a sack of tuna that was tied to the bait cage. (He got the cord, too.) A hungry female swam right into his mouth!

ready to run into some good-smelling food. Instead they ran into each other!"

Eugenie was at 3,800 feet, off Bermuda. It was to be her longest dive yet — seventeen and a half hours. But the hours seemed like minutes as she watched the oversized creatures. That day she saw twenty-one sharks of six species. Cramped in the small submersible, Eugenie wrote furiously in her notebook, describing everything.

On all her sub dives — in Bermuda, in Japan, in California, and in other places around the world — she made notes about creatures never before seen up close, so deep: snub-nose eels that burrow into the body of their prey, eating it from the inside out; deep-sea gulpers that look like snakes with huge heads and hinged mouths that open like a garbage truck to swallow their prey; a female silver shark releasing her eggs.

Eugenie kept notes and drew pictures of the strange species. A cat shark, seven feet long, was filmed for the first time; so was a cusk eel that looked like a white phantom in slow motion. A flying elephant, with gigantic ears, was actually a hooded octopus. The fins on its head looked like big ears — Eugenie nick-named it Dumbo.

Eugenie's notebook filled with descriptions of odd creatures: large bright red deepwater shrimps, with enormously long antennae, like a weird bunch of carrots; anglerfish that sometimes attack prey that is larger than themselves.

She saw strange small sea creatures, too. A sea dandelion, looking like a tiny burst of fireworks, clung to a rock spur 730 feet down. This four-inch gorgonian stings small prey with its tufted tentacles and then eats them.

A huge fifteen-foot elephant-ear sponge was the biggest sponge ever seen. "Marine life at that depth is well protected," Eugenie wrote in her notebook. "Even if a hurricane was raging at the surface, the elephant-ear sponge wouldn't budge."

There's so much to study, she thought. The small lantern shark that would fit into the palm of my hand. And the biggest fish ever seen in the deep sea, the sleeper shark. At twenty-three feet, the sleeper shark is the size of a city bus.

Eugenie remembered a cameraman's excitement when he first saw the sleeper shark. "We saw a fish bump into a wall. The sub shook! Then the wall moved! That wall was the shark!"

She recorded many firsts on her dives in the deep, deep sea. "It makes me realize that there

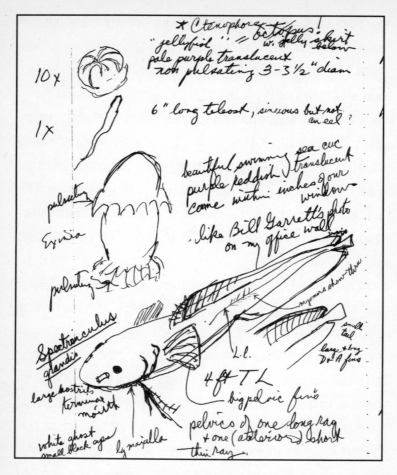

A page from Eugenie Clark's notebooks

Some of the creatures Eugenie saw in the waters off Japan include a large brotulid (fish). In her notebook, she describes the fish: "...white as a ghost, small black eyes...moving very slowly, not disturbed by lights."

are lots of things — big things — that we don't know about. There will always be more to learn. Always more surprises on these submersible dives."

Once she saw a red blob, as startling as a splash of blood. As the sub came closer, Eugenie saw the blob lift slightly and glide over the ledge without leaving a trail. Picking up speed, it shot into open water. Eugenie saw it was a squid over a foot long. She watched it swim up, with its tentacles down, rippling its mantle like a Spanish dancer.

One of her biggest surprises was when she saw the twenty-inch, cigar-shaped, green-eyed cookie-cutter shark. At night it swims up to the surface to attack large fish, even dolphins and whales. The cookie-cutter gets its teeth tightly into its victim. When its prey tries to get away, the cookie-cutter hangs on and twists its body around in a circle. It pulls a "cookie" — a plug of skin and flesh — out of the body of its victim.

Diving in submersibles raised new questions. Why do sharks rarely — if ever — go deeper than 7,000 feet? From the submersibles, new depth records were made. A tiger shark was found at 1,000 feet; a mako shark at 3,000 feet. But on four of the deepest dives, up to 12,000 feet, they didn't see any sharks. There are lots of their deep-sea relatives, the chimeras, at that depth. But why not sharks?

What are the effects of bright lights on the creatures? Eugenie saw that many of the sea creatures were attracted to the lights. Some seemed to go crazy, tumbling and zigzagging this way and that. Once a herd of fish became a meal for a moray eel. The fish were drawn to the lights. And the moray eel was drawn to the fish! Emory Kristof said, "It's as if someone hung out a sign saying, 'Eat here.'"

Another unsolved mystery is the megamouth, one of the largest deep-sea sharks in the world and one of the least understood. By 1996, only ten megamouths had been found.

In 1990, a fifteen-footer was accidentally caught in a fisherman's net. Small radio transmitters were implanted in its body so that scientists could tell its depth and location. It was videotaped underwater. The gentle giant that feeds on plankton actually allowed divers and photographers to come close, even to touch its enormous mouth.

After two days of intense studying, the scientists and photographers let the shark go on its way. Thanks to the radio transmitters, they made some important discoveries about the shark's movements: It swims near the surface at night and sinks to the deep water when the sun comes up — just like the plankton it feeds on!

In November 1994, the first female megamouth was discovered on a beach in Japan and was quickly frozen at a nearby aquarium. Three months later, Eugenie was invited to help other scientists dissect it. It continues to be studied.

Eugenie wonders what other fantastic creatures could live in the deep.

Could there really be a giant ocean squid so huge that just one sucker of one of its tentacles could cover the entire window of the submersible? No one has ever seen this monster squid alive. Scientists have proof it exists and is at least sixty feet long, bigger than a railroad car. Emory's wildest dream is to film it for the world to see. Eugenie would love to see it living in the depths, too. What else could make those dinner-plate-size marks found on whales? What else could leave pieces of strange, long tentacles found washed ashore on a beach?

What else lurks down there? In New Zealand, the mysterious remains of a giant creature with a small head, long neck, and flippers were found. It looked like a *plesiosaur,* the massive sea reptile that lived in dinosaur days. But after careful examination, the experts discovered the animal had been a basking shark.

Huge jellylike blobs weighing a ton were washed ashore. These "globsters" were a mystery until scientists finally determined they were from the skin of a whale — the part called the collagen layer.

Thanks to submersibles and remotely operated cameras, Eugenie and other scientists can explore, study, and make videos and pictures of the strange and fascinating creatures of the deep, deep sea.

FAMOUS EUGENIE CLARK

Eugenie has lived in the same house in Bethesda, Maryland, for more than thirty years. There are pictures of fish all around the house. She dries her dishes with dish towels that have patterns of sharks. She has fish-shaped candles, shark pillows, and pot holders, even a fish-shaped corkscrew. Pictures of her family and friends are everywhere. It is a warm and friendly house, just like its owner, Eugenie Clark.

12
Grandma Genie

Eugenie's grandson, Eli, is a lucky boy. Sometimes he gets to go with his grandma on her diving trips. When he was five years old, he took an underwater picture while he was snorkeling of a whale shark in Mexico. His picture was published in *National Geographic* in June 1997.

Sometimes one or more of Eugenie's four children take time from their busy lives to come along on her scuba-diving expeditions.

Her oldest daughter, Hera, remembers her childhood as being very normal. "When I was growing up, it never occurred to me that my childhood was unusual," she says. "All of us kids could swim before we could walk. I was scuba diving when I was four years old. To us it was perfectly natural to grow up helping our mother catch twelve-foot sharks from a fourteen-foot boat and to spend hours dissecting them in the lab."

Eugenie gazed out her window to the Japanese garden she and her stepfather had designed together. When he died in 1992, he was almost ninety-two. She missed him so much. Eugenie remembered how her stepfather liked to stand on the little bridge over the pond and ring a bell, the signal for the fish in the pond to swim to a special rock for food. Eugenie had trained the goldfish to respond to the sound of a bell, a method practiced in Japan for two thousand years.

Eugenie and her children still feel more comfortable using chopsticks than forks. She was brought up by her Japanese mother and her Japanese stepfather, whom she called Pop. She never knew her English father, who died when she was a baby.

Pop had lived to see baby Eli, his first great-grandchild.

Eugenie flies to Florida often to visit Eli. He loves the stories his grandmother tells him. "More talking fishes, Neenee," he said to her when he was two years old, fascinated by Eugenie's true adventure stories about sharks and other creatures of the sea.

Everyone loves Eugenie's stories. Every year she gives dozens of lectures. She's invited to speak all over the world.

Eugenie hoped she would have more time at home after she retired as a professor of zoology at the University of Maryland. But her life is busier than ever.

Her research and dive trips continue. Most summers find her in the Red Sea or the South Pacific. She still teaches one course a year in the fall, "Sea Monsters and Deep-Sea Sharks." She shows films and slides of her real-life adventures beneath the sea. Her students, ranging from a nine-year-old girl to grandmothers in their eighties, say Eugenie's course is one of the most popular at the university.

Even though Eugenie has retired, she spends many hours at her lab and in her small office at the university. Her desk is piled high with letters asking her to write articles and books and to give lectures and interviews. She's written more than 150 articles and has participated in twenty-four television specials about the sea. She's discovered eleven species of fish, and four more have been named in her honor. She has won seven medals and twenty other awards for her work in marine biology, conservation, and writing. She has three honorary doctorate degrees from three different universities.

She gets thousands of letters from children. The children ask her many questions. "Are you ever afraid of anything?" they want to know.

"No shark has ever scared me," Eugenie says. "The only thing I've ever been afraid of is being alone in the dark. It started when I was a very young child, listening to my Japanese grandmother's wonderful and scary ghost stories."

Many people are happy to share Eugenie's experiences, especially her new husband, whom she married a few months after her seventy-fifth birthday in 1997.

"I have the most interesting life of anybody I know," she says. "I don't dive as many times a day as I used to but I still like to make two-hour scuba dives."

To keep fit, Eugenie exercises at the local YMCA when she's not traveling.

"I used to say I'll keep diving till I'm ninety. But why stop then? I hope to keep diving, studying, and sharing my knowledge and excitement about the sea and its creatures that I love so much as long as I live."

Eugenie studies a six-gill frill shark. She will never lose her curiosity about the creatures of the sea.

13
Eugenie Makes a Movie

Eugenie was used to being in front of cameras. By 1992, she had appeared in twenty-four television shows. But this IMAX movie, *In Search of the Great Sharks,* was different. The special IMAX cameras and their huge forty-foot screens (the height of a four-story building) make moviegoers feel they are underwater.

Eugenie knew that this IMAX film would be so different from the movie *Jaws.* In *Jaws,* the filmmakers used a big plastic great white shark and a small boat with small people so that the shark appeared huge. They put short people in the shark cage so that the shark would look even more enormous.

The filming of *In Search of the Great Sharks* began in 1991. Eugenïe flew to Dangerous Reef in Australia. One of her students, Karen Moody, was invited, too. Karen had never seen a live shark except in the aquarium. She had dissected dead sharks with Eugenie in the lab. Now she'd be diving with the most dreaded sharks in the world.

The IMAX moviemakers used "movie magic" tricks for the shark cage. Instead of cages made of steel, their cages were made out of clear transparent plastic that give movie-goers the feeling that the divers are in the open seas with the great white sharks — as though the shark cages weren't there at all!

Eugenie and Karen were in one cage together. Suddenly a great white shark rushed toward them and bumped the front of the cage hard. Eugenie glanced at Karen to see how she was taking her first encounter. But Karen was nowhere to be seen. Where was she? There was no way Karen could have left the cage. The trapdoor on the top wasn't open.

Eugenie looked to the right and to the left. Then she looked down. There was Karen, on her hands and knees between Eugenie's legs. (Eventually Karen got to feel comfortable with great whites swimming around her, just like Eugenie.)

Diving with great white sharks was tame compared to what happened next with blue sharks. Eugenie and shark expert Rodney Fox were diving with blue sharks off Catalina Island in California. The movie people wanted Eugenie to put on a chain-mail suit for protection. But Eugenie knew how to act around the sharks. She didn't like to wear the heavy suit.

Rodney wore the chain-mail suit at the director's request. The scene was set. Eugenie would come from one direction, Rodney from another. They were supposed to meet at the baited cage where dozens of blue sharks would surround them.

There was a current running in the sea, so they planned to make a "drift dive." In a drift dive, the photographers, the cage with the bait to attract the sharks, and the boat above drift along with the current. Eugenie and Rodney dove thirty feet below and drifted along, too. The waters beneath them plunged down to 3,000 feet.

Eugenie and Rodney had on Scubafone helmets, which served as both face mask and phone, so that they could talk and listen to each other.

As they had planned, Eugenie swam to the bait cage. But there was no sign of Rodney. Then Eugenie heard Rodney's chilling words on the Scubafone, "Help! I'm in trouble!"

"Where are you?" Eugenie asked. "Rodney, what's the matter?"

There was no answer. Eugenie spoke urgently to the people on the boat. "Rodney's not here. I don't see him anywhere in the water. There's only one direction he could have gone. Down."

Down meant 3,000 feet. And 3,000 feet meant death.

Rodney's wife, Kay, was on the boat. Eugenie could imagine how terrified Kay was feeling. Over and over again, the captain called Rodney on the Scubafone. There was no reply.

Suddenly the captain of the boat shouted, "There he is!" He pointed to a figure far from the boat.

Rodney was hauled out of the water, alive but exhausted. He was no longer wearing his Scubafone.

He gasped out his story. "I was swimming along when one of my flippers came off. I saw the flipper begin to sink. Without thinking, I dove down to get it. I should have known better. My dive suit compressed. Then the chain-mail suit acted like an anchor. Down I went. The deeper I went, the faster I dropped. I reached for my inflator hose, which would bring me back to the surface, but it was caught in all the extra gear I was wearing."

Everyone fell silent, thinking how close Rodney had come to death. He went on with his story. "With my last bit of reason, I began taking my equipment off. When I pulled off the helmet, I found my inflator hose and I could inflate air into my vest. I came up, probably too fast."

Without his helmet, Rodney couldn't breathe in, but he let out the pressurized air from his lungs as he rose and prevented worse problems.

Rodney was rushed to the hospital. Eugenie thought it was a miracle that he was okay. "You couldn't get me into one of those suits," Eugenie said. "Rodney's experience was an example of danger from human error and equipment, not from sharks."

In one scene from the movie, a blue shark is biting Rodney's arm. To make the shark come to him, Rodney first pulled a dead fish over his arm.

"I know that you practically have to shove your elbow in the blue shark's mouth to get it to bite you," Eugenie said. "The shark only bit Rodney because it smelled the dead fish. The director wanted a dramatic scene, but you really have to coax the shark to bite you. Blue sharks get longer than ten feet. We did not film any ten-footers. Most were small, six to eight feet — but the IMAX cameras make them look much bigger."

The movie opened in 1993 and millions of people went to see it.

Eugenie hopes that the film made people more aware of the wonders of sharks and that they will appreciate the sharks' place in the oceans of the world.

A Letter from Eugenie Clark

Dear Girls and Boys,

I consider myself very lucky because my work combines my two favorite childhood hobbies, watching fishes and diving under the water.

I loved school, except taking exams, of course, but even that got to be a challenging game after a while. I had wonderful teachers who taught me that math, statistics, chemistry, physics, and geology were as important as biology to understand fishes and to become an *ichthyologist,* a scientist who specializes in fishes. My English and speech courses gave me a chance to share with others my fascination with fishes. One of my English teachers told me, "I don't know how you do it. No matter what topic I assign the class to write about, you always manage to bring in a fish!" My teacher almost always gave me an A or an A–. She said I had to learn to spell better.

I enjoy my new husband, great friendships, and the joy of having four children and my first grandchild. I think about how the world will be when he grows up.

A big concern of mine is the deterioration of some of the world's most beautiful and valuable underwater habitats, especially the coral reefs.

Some reefs and the fishes that live there are being saved through marine parks and sanctuaries. I'm encouraged to see these breakthroughs, but there is still much conservation work to be done. Through the study of marine ecology, we are learning how animals and plants interact and relate to their environment. The sea and its creatures must be understood as part of our planet. My students at the University of Maryland understand this need for saving all creatures, even sharks.

So many young people write me about their fascination with sharks. Very few people are ever attacked by sharks. It's safer to dive with sharks than to drive in a car. Millions of sharks are being killed by people every year. Sharks should be more afraid of us than we are of them.

All of us, including those in the field of medicine, have a lot to learn from sharks. Sharks have one of the most remarkable immune systems in the animal kingdom. In their natural habitat, they can ward off almost any disease.

I hope this book makes you more aware of the wonders of all sea creatures, sharks, too. I hope that you, like me, will learn to appreciate their role in our oceans and want to protect them.

Your Friend,

Eugenie Clark

Bethesda, Maryland

Written by Eugenie Clark

Eugenie Clark has written hundreds of articles for magazines. Interested readers may want to look up some of these stories in back issues of *National Geographic*.

"Into the Lairs of 'Sleeping' Sharks" *April 1975*

"Strange World of Red Sea Reefs" *September 1975*

"The Red Sea's Flashlight Fish" *November 1978*

"Sharks: Magnificent and Misunderstood" *August 1981*

"Hidden Life of an Undersea Desert in the Red Sea" *July 1983*

"The World of Sharks at 2,000 Feet" *November 1986*

"Dispatches from a Distant World" *October 1990*

"Whale Sharks: Gentle Monsters of the Deep" *December 1992*